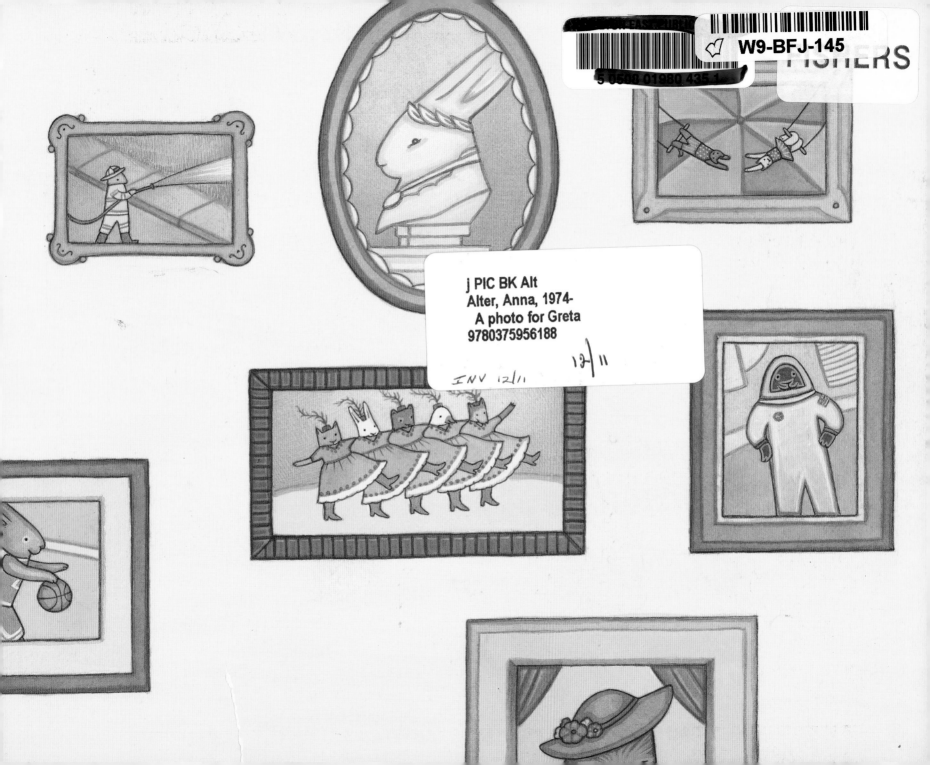

For my dad

THIS IS A BORZOI BOOK PUBLISHED BY ALFRED A. KNOPF

Copyright © 2011 by Anna Alter

All rights reserved. Published in the United States by Alfred A. Knopf,
an imprint of Random House Children's Books, a division of Random House, Inc., New York.

Knopf, Borzoi Books, and the colophon are registered trademarks of Random House, Inc.

Visit us on the Web! www.randomhouse.com/kids

Educators and librarians, for a variety of teaching tools, visit us at www.randomhouse.com/teachers

Library of Congress Cataloging-in-Publication Data is available upon request.
ISBN 978-0-375-85618-1 (trade) — ISBN 978-0-375-95618-8 (lib. bdg.)

The illustrations in this book were created using acrylic paint.

MANUFACTURED IN MALAYSIA
May 2011
10 9 8 7 6 5 4 3 2 1
First Edition
Random House Children's Books supports the First Amendment and celebrates the right to read.

A Photo for Greta

by Anna Alter

ALFRED A. KNOPF

NEW YORK

Greta loves her dad.

She loves to play checkers with him in the park after school.

She loves to get ice cream together on Saturdays.

But most of all, Greta loves to look at her dad's pictures.

Greta's dad works as a photographer. He travels all around the world taking pictures of very important people.

Sometimes Greta wishes she were an opera star or a famous astronaut so that she could be in his pictures, too.

One day he was out taking pictures at the circus.
Greta thought of all the things her dad would see.

Then she got an idea.

When her dad got home, he scooped her up.
"Are you going to join the circus?" he asked.

"Yes," said Greta. "Will you take my picture?"

"But of course," he said.

The next day, her dad was out taking pictures at the ballet.
She could imagine all the ballerinas twirling gracefully.

So she got out her tutu.

When her dad got home, he scooped her up.
"Are you going to join the ballet?" he asked.

"Yes," said Greta. "Will you take my picture?"

"Absolutely," he said.

The following afternoon,
Greta hopped on her mom's back.
"Where is Dad today?" asked Greta.

"He is out taking pictures of a country music band," said her mom.
"He won't be home until after you are asleep."

Greta plucked a sad and lonely tune on her guitar.

When it was time to go to bed, Greta wished her dad were there to tuck her in. So her mom took out the photo album.

That night, Greta dreamt that she was a photographer, too.

In the morning, Greta's dad scooped her up. "Howdy, cowgirl," he said.

"One day I'm going to have an important job, like you," said Greta.

"You already do," said her dad. "Your job is to be my Greta, and that is the most important job there is."

Greta's dad lifted her onto his shoulders, then put her down right in front of his camera.

It was the best day she could remember.

ACTIVITIES

❀ Make your own photo album! Greta's dad takes many pictures of people who are important to him. What and who is important to you? Take a picture of three people or things that are important to you and glue the pictures into a notebook. Then write a paragraph next to each picture about why you chose it.

❀ Conduct a job interview! Greta's dad is a photographer. What does your mom or dad do for a job? Make a list of questions about your parents' jobs and then interview them. What do they like about their jobs? What kinds of things do they learn about at work? What are some of the activities they do at their jobs?

❀ Make a daily photo journal! Spend a week taking pictures of one thing you do each day. At the end of the week, glue them into a notebook. Then list three details about each activity next to the pictures.

❀ Study a photographer! Go on a trip to your local library and research some different photographers. What types of things do they like to take pictures of? What makes their pictures unique? Try taking some pictures in their style.

First Grade